To my son, Tony—

your calling is to spread God's love to various cultures. You always make me laugh, even when situations in life get tough. Your potential is limitless and your drive unmatched. Just remember, if all the sons in the world were lined up, I'd still pick you!

www.mascotbooks.com

Celebrate Diversity

For more information, please contact:
Mascot Books
620 Herndon Parkway, Suite 320
Herndon, VA 20170
info@mascotbooks.com

Library of Congress Control Number: 2020918346

CPSIA Code: PRT0121A
ISBN-13: 978-1-64543-661-4

Printed in the United States

Celebrate Diversity

Dawn Marie Thompson

Illustrated by Oana Cocheci &
Ferencz Erzsebet

In Sattler Elementary's fourth grade class,
Each child is special, whether they fail or pass.

Come with me, and we'll look inside,
At each child in school who does reside.

Each child is different, no one can compare.
They have different clothes, skin, eyes, and hair.

Together they learn from eight until three.
They study math, reading, and history.

James has a head wrap on his head,
While Ella prefers a ball cap that's red.

Sofia likes a tam for a hat,
While Luke's kofia is where it's at...

Some observe
Christmas as a
way of life,

Others Hanukkah
with candles of light.

Some celebrate birthdays with a cake that is tall.

And some observe nothing at all.

Jacob is short, and Mia is tall.
Evan is thin, and John not at all.

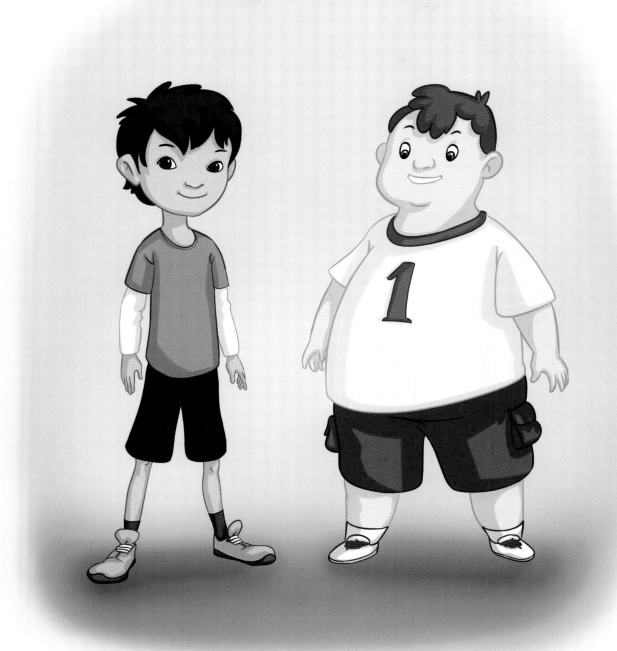

Their shapes are all different, and that's okay.
They are each special in their own way.

Some listen to music with a lot of drums.
Others like to paint or dance to have fun.

Wyatt plays the trumpet and Charlotte the flute,
Lincoln the guitar and a trombone to boot.

Some live in families with lots of folks.

Ben lives with his sister who always jokes.

Sam with his mom,

Jamal his dad,

And Maria with all the
brothers she has.

Some in this class are from the U.S.A.
Others are from countries much farther away.

There are kids from Sudan and one from Peru,
Alex from Nepal and Tazeen from Beirut.

Olivia lives in a house
made of brick.

And Johnny's in an apartment, and so is Mick.

Terrance lives on a farm with animals around.

Sydney's home is a trailer, where her family's found.

Skylar's good at sports, a ball in each hand,
Kathy travels across various lands.

Tony plays games, and Hailey likes to cook.
Each skill is different, none to be overlooked.

The kids at the school are special, it's true.
They are all unique in what they do.

None of them look quite the same,
But to this one school they all came.

Unlike or the same, it matters none.
Make friends at school while having fun!

Celebrate others and learn from them too,
Enjoy other people who are different from you.

It's the kindness we share that matters the most.
It's the respect we show to other folks.
It's looking at others for what's inside.
It's those we learn to walk alongside.

How We Should Treat Each Other

1. Accept the differences in one another.
2. Value the opinions of others.
3. Learn about each other's differences.
4. Listen to one another.
5. Respect each other.
6. Celebrate diversity!

Remember: differences are part of what make us special.

Words for Parents About Diversity

1. Children notice differences at a young age, and teaching cultural differences will increase their awareness.

2. Daily interactions help shape children's perspectives and will improve their critical thinking skills.

3. Cultural education helps build young children's self-confidence and skills.

4. Diversity helps boost creativity and helps develop problem-solving abilities.

5. Learning about culture helps children understand the world around them and develop cognitive abilities.

6. Children learn from the situations they witness in which discrimination takes place.

7. Try to be a great role model!

Let's all do better for our world.

About the Author

Dawn Marie Thompson is a writer, speaker, and ordained minister. She currently works at a child welfare agency that helps children throughout the world. She has given birth to three children and has been a mentor to many others. Her heart for children is to help them have as wonderful of a childhood as the one she experienced. She enjoys teaching kids the life skills necessary to live a full, abundant life. Dawn has served on several boards and committees to better the communities in which she has lived. She has helped to organize and operate teen centers and has developed mentoring and training programs for volunteers.